THE JIM FOREST READERS

Jim Forest

and

Dead Man's Peak

JOHN and NANCY RAMBEAU

Illustrations by VIOLA FRENCH

HARR WAGNER PUBLISHING COMPANY • San Francisco

TABLE of CONTENTS

The Red Mountain

"What can be keeping Uncle Don?" Jim thought.

It was very late. The ranger had been gone for a long time.

Jim went to the door. He looked down the road. He could not see the ranger's truck.

The sun was going down. The mountains looked red in the sunlight. The snow on Dead

Man's Peak looked red. Jim had heard many things about Dead Man's Peak. He thought of them now, as he looked at the mountain.

Jim heard the telephone ring. He ran to answer it.

"Big Pines Ranger Station. Jim Forest talking," he said.

A man said, "I must talk to the ranger."

"I am sorry. The ranger is not here now. He should be back very soon," Jim answered.

"I must talk to him. Have him call me as soon as he comes in," said the man. He gave Jim a number for the ranger to call.

Jim put the number down on a paper. He put the paper on the table. Just then, he heard the forest ranger's truck.

Jim ran to the door. He saw Ranger Don get out of the truck.

"Jim!" his uncle called. "Sorry to be so late. Help me with these boxes, will you?"

Jim ran down the steps. "What do you have in all the boxes?" he asked.

"Help me bring them in. You will find out," said Ranger Don.

Jim ran up the steps with the boxes. He put them on the table.

"Well, open them up. They are for you," said his uncle.

"For me?" Jim said. "Oh, boy!"

Jim opened the boxes as fast as he could.

"Snowshoes! Boots! All these warm clothes! They will be just right when winter comes," Jim said.

"You need these things now, Jim. I want you to go with me on a patrol trip," Ranger Don said.

Jim had been on many patrol trips with his uncle. It was part of the ranger's job to patrol Big Pines. Jim looked at the clothes again. They were all warm, winter things. But it was not winter now.

"We—we must be going into the snow," Jim said slowly.

Jim knew of only one place where there was snow now. And that was Dead Man's Peak!

Ranger Don was looking at the big map on the wall.

"Come over here to the map, Jim. I'll show you where we are going," he said.

Jim watched the ranger's hand move across the map.

"Oh, oh! I was afraid of that. We are going to Dead Man's Peak," Jim said.

His uncle laughed. "Don't be afraid of a name, Jim. If I thought there were danger,

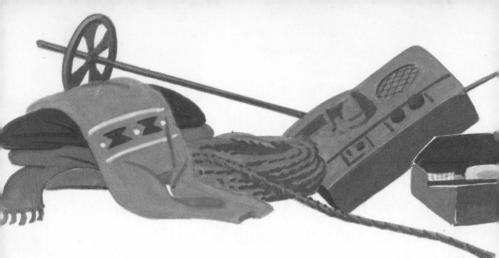

I would not take you. We are not going all the way up the mountain. We will only go as far as the patrol cabin," he said.

"Will we get into the deep snow?" Jim asked.

"The patrol cabin is below the snow, now. But anything can happen at this time of year. We could get into some snow up there," Ranger Don said. "We will need to pack tonight."

Jim took the boxes from the table. He put them in the fire. The ranger got his field kit ready. In the field kit were all the things a forest ranger needed.

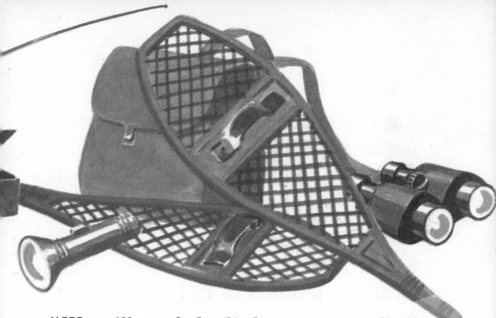

"We will need the little two-way radio," said Ranger Don.

The ranger helped Jim pack the things he would need for the trip.

"Keep your pack light. We will go almost all the way on foot," he said.

At last all the packing was done. Jim and his uncle sat down to eat. All at once, Jim thought of the telephone call. He jumped up.

"Oh, Uncle Don! I just thought of something. A man called when you were gone. He wanted you to call back," he said.

Jim ran to the table. He could not find the paper with the number on it. He looked and looked. But the paper was gone!

"Oh, Uncle Don! I must have put the paper in the fire with the boxes," Jim said.

"Did he tell you what he wanted?" asked Ranger Don.

"No, he just said he had to talk to you," said Jim.

"Well, then there is nothing to do but wait. If the man wants to talk to me that much, he will call back."

Ranger Don put his arm around the boy. "Don't worry," he said.

But the telephone did not ring again.

And Jim did worry. He did not sleep well that night. He thought about the telephone call. He thought about the trip to Dead Man's Peak. He thought about the great mountain covered with red snow.

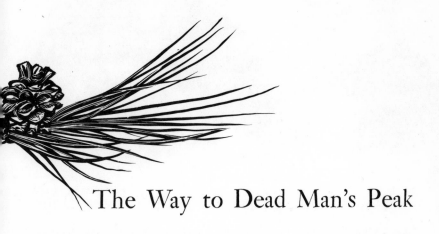

The Way to Dead Man's Peak

There was no sun that morning. A cold wind came down from Dead Man's Peak. Jim knew that the snow would not be long in coming. His hands were cold as he went to get the horses.

"Are Star and Big Boy ready?" the ranger asked.

"Yes," Jim called back.

"Good! Let's go then," said Ranger Don.
He ran down the steps and jumped on Star.
Jim climbed on Big Boy, and they rode down
the hill. They rode by Pete's store. Pete came
out to talk to them.

"We are going across the valley to Dead
Man's Peak," the ranger said. "We are going
by the mill. Is there anything you want me
to take?"

"You could take these letters to Mr. Higgins, ranger," Pete said. He gave some letters
to Ranger Don.

Jim and his uncle started across the main road. They cut through the forest and down into the valley.

"There is a logging road around here," the ranger said. "Let's cut over and find it. It will take us right to the mill."

Jim could see where the logging men had been working.

"They did not take many trees here, Uncle Don," he said.

"No, Jim. A long time ago there was a fire here. It took many years for the trees to come up again. This year there were only a few trees ready to be cut. Soon, there will be more," said the ranger.

"There is the logging road!" Jim said.

"Good," said Ranger Don.

They turned into the logging road. The horses flew over the ground. Soon they came to the mill.

There were some small cabins near the mill. The Higgins family lived in one of the cabins. Jim and the ranger rode up to the Higgins' cabin.

Mr. Higgins heard the horses and came out.

"Glad to see you, ranger," he said.

"It's good to see you, too," said Ranger Don. "We went by Pete's store, and here are some letters for you. Is Joe here?"

"Joe! Come here, son," Mr. Higgins called.

Joe came out of the cabin. He said hello to Jim and his uncle.

"How would you like a job, Joe?" Ranger Don asked. "Would you take care of Star and Big Boy for us? We are going up the mountain on a patrol trip."

"Well, I—all right, ranger. I'll take care of the horses," Joe said. "Are you going up to Dead Man's Peak—right now?"

"Yes, we are, Joe," the ranger said. He climbed down from Star.

Jim jumped off Big Boy, and Joe took the horses.

Jim watched the other boy take the horses away.

"What is wrong with Joe? He is afraid of something. What can it be?" Jim thought. Joe used to be friendly. But he did not seem very friendly now.

"Now Joe will have two jobs," said Mr. Higgins. "Some boys asked him to watch their car. They gave him ten dollars."

13

"That is a lot of money for watching a car!" said Ranger Don.

"I thought it was too much money," Mr. Higgins said. "There were three boys. They came here this morning. They said they just wanted to look around."

"Hmmm," said the ranger. "Do you know their names? Do you know where they live?"

"They are staying at Big Pines Lodge, ranger. One of the boys is named Andy Bangs. The car is his," said Mr. Higgins.

"Andy Bangs," said Ranger Don slowly. "I have heard that name. I think the boy must be Bob Bangs' son. The Bangs family has a lot of money."

"Maybe so. But I wish Joe had not taken that ten dollars," Mr. Higgins said.

"I wish I knew where the boys had gone," the ranger said. "I hope they did not try to climb Dead Man's Peak."

"But, Uncle Don! They would have asked at the ranger station. No one would climb Dead Man's Peak without asking the ranger," Jim said. "No one could be that foolish."

"I hope you are right, Jim," said Ranger Don. "Come on. It's time we started. It's a long way to the patrol cabin."

Jim and the ranger said good-by to Mr. Higgins and started off. Jim turned and saw Joe Higgins standing by the cabin, looking at them.

"It's funny that Joe did not say good-by to us," Jim thought.

Ranger Don looked up at the mountain.

"I'll be glad when this job is done, Jim. Winter is not far away. And Dead Man's Peak is no place to be when winter comes."

They started up the trail.

Far away, a long, black car came along the main road. The car slowed down and turned up the road to Big Pines Ranger Station. There it stopped.

A small, heavy man jumped out and ran up the steps. He banged on the door and waited. He banged again. Then he shook the door.

"Gone!" he said. His hands dropped. He turned and looked across the valley to Dead Man's Peak. There was fear in his eyes.

"I must find that forest ranger," he said. "I must find him before it's too late!"

Three Boys Lost

Jim looked back. The mill and the cabins were black dots in the valley far below.

"Is the cabin far from here?" he asked.

"The patrol cabin is up there—just below the snow," said the ranger.

It was hard going now. In some places logs lay across the trail. Jim and the ranger stopped to move the logs.

"I like to keep these trails open," Ranger Don said. "We may want to get back down in a hurry!"

Jim stopped. He was looking at something on the trail.

"Look here, Uncle Don. A paper bag! It looks like someone was eating here—and not too long ago."

The ranger took the bag. He turned it over.

"You are right, Jim. This bag has not been here long. But no one should be climbing Dead Man's Peak at this time of year. And

no one should come up here without first asking me!" the ranger said.

Jim thought of the car they had seen at the cabin. He thought of Joe. Something had been wrong down there. What was it?

"Those boys! Andy Bangs and the others. Would they try to climb Dead Man's Peak?" Jim asked.

His uncle said slowly, "I don't know. Those boys must have been told that they had to ask me first. They would have found that out at Big Pines Lodge."

The ranger took the pack from his back. He opened his field kit and took out his field glasses. For a long time he looked through the glasses.

"Hallooo! Hallooo, up there!" he called.

There was no answer.

"Maybe they ate here and went back down the mountain," Jim said.

Ranger Don looked at the trail. "I can see where the boys went up, Jim," he said. "But, if they came back down, they did not use this trail. Come on. Let's get up to the patrol cabin. It will be dark soon."

Jim helped to pack the field kit again. They started off. The ranger moved fast. Jim found it hard to keep up with him. They both hoped that they would find the boys safe in the patrol cabin. When they came to the cabin, no one was there.

Ranger Don went to the telephone. Jim heard him put in a call to Big Pines Lodge.

Jim looked around the little cabin. It was much like others he had seen in Big Pines Forest. It was made to stand the winter snows. In it were a stove, table and chairs, lamps, and two beds. Blankets were put up on wires about the room. This would keep them safe from rats. In the floor of the cabin was a small door. Under the floor, there was a place to keep food.

There was work to be done before dark. Jim got wood for the stove.

The ranger put down the telephone. "The boys left Big Pines Lodge this morning, and they are not back. They had talked about climbing Dead Man's Peak. The man at the lodge told them to ask me first."

"They knew you would not let them go," Jim said.

"They started about four hours before us, Jim. They are up in the snow by this time. I will go after them in the morning," he said.

It had been a long, hard climb. Jim and his uncle were both tired. After eating, they went to bed.

Jim was just going to sleep. He heard a sound. At first he thought he was just hearing things. Then he sat up and shook his head. There it was again.

"OoooooooOOOOOOH."

Jim thought of all he had heard about Dead Man's Peak. He thought of the men that had been lost there, long ago.

Jim went cold all over. He called, "Uncle Don! Uncle Don! There is some-one out there."

The Climb Begins

Ranger Don sat up and shook his head. Jim ran to the door and pulled it open.

"Halloooo—ooooooOOOOH—ooooOOOH."

The sound was all around the cabin. It seemed to come from the snow-covered peaks above. Jim looked into the black night. Then he saw the lights. They seemed very small and far away.

"Uncle Don, do you think it's the boys?" Jim asked.

"We will see. Hurry, Jim," the ranger said. "Light the lamp and bring it to the door." Then he called through his hands. "Hallooo, Hallooo, down there."

The lights moved closer and closer. At last Jim could make out two shapes in the dark.

"It's Higgins! Someone is with him," said Ranger Don.

At last the two men reached the cabin. Jim closed the door against the cold wind. He put more wood on the stove. Then he put on the coffee.

"This is Bob Bangs, ranger," Mr. Higgins said. He sat down on the bed and pulled off his boots. "I tried to tell him to wait at the cabin. He would not do it."

Mr. Bangs sat down, too. "I—I had to come. My boy is up here," he said. "He and those

other boys are not used to mountain climbing, ranger. They were foolish to try it. When I found out, it was too late to stop them."

Bob Bangs was small and heavy. He was not made for mountain climbing. Jim did not see how he had reached the patrol cabin.

"Did you telephone last night?" the ranger asked.

"Yes. But I did not wait for you to call back. I left right away," Mr. Bangs said.

"But how did you know we were on Dead Man's Peak?" asked the ranger.

"I looked for you at the ranger station. A man at the store told me you were here. Mr. Higgins said he would bring me to the patrol cabin," said Mr. Bangs.

28

Mr. Higgins looked down at his hands. "I know this mountain, ranger," he said. "You may need help in finding those boys."

"Higgins, you don't get money for this work. I do. And you have a family down there," Ranger Don said.

"I will give you anything. Just bring back my son!" said Mr. Bangs.

Mr. Higgins shook his head. "My boy Joe did something wrong. That ten dollars he took—it was not just for watching the car. The boys gave him the money to keep still. He knew they were coming up here."

"So that is why Joe was not friendly," the ranger said slowly. "If I had only been told this morning."

Mr. Higgins went on, "Joe did not stop to think of the danger. But he knows now. If something should happen to those boys, it would trouble Joe all his life."

Ranger Don went to the telephone. He called the main ranger station.

"I am up on Dead Man's Peak at the patrol cabin. I am going to need a helicopter up here first thing in the morning. Three boys are up there on the peak. We have to get them down. How about it? Can you send the helicopter?" he asked.

Jim watched the ranger's face. He knew then that something was wrong.

"I see. I see," the ranger was saying. "But look, the helicopter can spot the boys. There should be time for that. All right. Do what you can, will you?"

Ranger Don put down the telephone.

Mr. Bangs looked at the ranger. There was fear in his eyes.

"What is it?" he asked.

"They will send the helicopter," Ranger Don said. "But I don't know how long it can stay up here. There is a storm coming, Mr. Bangs. It will hit soon."

"But Andy and the boys—they will be up there in the storm!" said Mr. Bangs. "You must do something!"

"We will do the very best we can. The best thing we can do now is to get some sleep —all four of us," said Ranger Don.

There were just two beds in the cabin. Ranger Don wanted Mr. Bangs to sleep in one of them. Mr. Higgins went to sleep in the other. The ranger took a blanket and lay down by the stove near Jim.

The night seemed very long. It was still dark when Jim heard the ranger moving around. Then Mr. Higgins was up, too.

Jim fixed something to eat. Mr. Bangs wanted to help. His hands shook, and he dropped things. Jim wanted to tell him to sit down. But he knew Mr. Bangs needed to be doing something. They ate and had coffee, waiting for morning to come.

Ranger Don went to the door and looked out. "I think we can start now, Higgins," he said. "It will soon be light. Take care of things here, Jim."

They took their things and started off. Jim and Mr. Bangs went to the door.

"Bring my boy back. I will give you any-thing—anything! Just bring Andy back," Mr. Bangs said.

Mr. Higgins looked at him. Then he looked up at Dead Man's Peak.

"I am not going up there for money, Mr. Bangs. I have a son, too," he said.

Both men shook hands with Mr. Bangs. Then they started off.

Help from a Helicopter

"I don't like the look of those clouds," Ranger Don said. He looked up at the peak above. Dark clouds were moving around the peak. The two men were well up into the snow now. The patrol cabin was only a small black dot below them. The valley seemed very far away.

"And I don't like the feel of this wind,"
Mr. Higgins said. "I hope that helicopter
comes soon. We will never spot those boys
without help."

The wind was strong and ice-cold. The two
men pushed hard against it. Both had snowshoes and dark glasses.

Ranger Don stopped. He took out some
rope. It was not heavy, but it was very strong.

"Here, take an end of this rope. Put it
around you. I'll have the other end around
me," he said.

Mr. Higgins put on the rope as he was told.
Then they started on again.

"There is a big snow field between those two small peaks. I think we will go that way," the ranger said. "But watch out! There are cracks in the ice. They may have been covered over by snow."

The ranger went first. He had a pole with him. Before each step, he tried the snow with the pole. At one place, the snow gave way under the pole. Ranger Don looked down. There was a deep crack by his feet.

"There is a big crack along here. I think we had better go over to the right," he said.

"I hope those boys knew what they were doing," Mr. Higgins said.

"Dead Man's Peak is not a bad climb," the ranger said. "But it is no place to be in a storm. We may be in for trouble."

They pushed on. The cold wind thundered about them.

"Ranger, the helicopter! Look up there," Higgins said.

The two men stopped.

There it was! A black dot was moving across the sky. Closer and closer came the helicopter. Ranger Don took out his radio.

"I hope this thing works," he said to Higgins. He called the helicopter. "This is Ranger Don Gray. We are down here on the snow field, between the two small peaks. Can you spot us?"

At first nothing came from the radio. Then the call came in from the helicopter.

"We have you spotted, ranger. We are going up to look for the boys. Stay where you are."

Higgins and Ranger Don were glad to stop for a time. But they soon found it was hard to keep warm sitting still.

They watched the little helicopter. It seemed to move slowly.

"Have you seen anything?" Ranger Don said into the radio.

"I am afraid not," the answer came back. "And we can't stay up here too long. We are picking up too much ice. Wait—hold on! There is something at the foot of the main peak. Watch for a flare."

The two men watched the helicopter. It flew down near the foot of the main peak. Then they saw a red spot of fire falling from the helicopter. It was the flare.

"They have spotted the boys. They are at the foot of that wall of rock," Higgins said.

Ranger Don waited. He listened to the radio. Then the call came from the helicopter.

"We spotted your boys, ranger. One of them seems to be all right. The other has taken a fall. He is down on a shelf in a deep crack. We are dropping a litter and first-aid things on the peak near those boys."

Ranger Don looked at Higgins. The ranger's face was white.

"But there were three boys. Where is the other boy? Can you see him?" he said into the radio.

"Sorry, ranger," the answer came back. "We see only two boys. This storm is going to hit soon. We are picking up a lot of ice. We must go back now. Go right up from where you are. You should reach the boys in a little over an hour."

The helicopter moved away from the peak. It went over the men on the snow field. Soon it was nothing but a black dot in the sky.

The two men looked at each other. They did not talk, but started across the snow field to the wall of rock. They thought of Mr. Bangs waiting in the patrol cabin below. One of the three boys was his son. Was Andy safe, or was he hurt? Or was Andy Bangs lost in the deep snows of Dead Man's Peak?

The Wait in the Storm

Jim looked at Mr. Bangs. He was standing in the door of the patrol cabin. He was looking up at Dead Man's Peak. He had stood there for hours. His hands were stiff with cold. He had watched Ranger Don and Higgins start up into the snow. Now they were far away. The helicopter had come and gone. But still Mr. Bangs stood, looking up at the snow-covered peak. Jim had tried to make him come in and sit down.

At last Jim said, "It's starting to snow. There is nothing we can see now. Maybe the men will be coming back soon. We should have the cabin warm, Mr. Bangs. Let's close the door and get the stove going again."

Mr. Bangs turned. Slowly he closed the door behind him.

"I think you are right, Jim. But it's so hard—just sitting here waiting." He sat down and put his head in his hands.

Jim knew there was little he could say to make Mr. Bangs feel better. Maybe if he could just keep him talking, it would help the time go by.

"I wanted life to be easy for Andy. I gave him too much. But I can see now—I did things all wrong. I wish I had found more time to be with Andy," Mr. Bangs said.

Jim worked to get the fire started. He made some coffee. Then he sat down by Mr. Bangs.

"Higgins and Uncle Don know this mountain well. They know just what to do up there. The men will do their best. They will bring your boy back, Mr. Bangs," he said.

"It's a funny thing, Jim," Mr. Bangs said. "I worked all my life to make money. But all the money in the world can not help my boy now. No one can help him but those two men—two men I never saw before."

A cold wind was thundering at the cabin door. Jim looked out. The snow blew around the cabin. The ground was covered with snow.

Jim put on his boots and snowshoes. He picked up a shovel.

"I am going to shovel some of that snow away from the door," he said. "And we are going to need more wood soon."

"I can help with the wood, Jim," Mr. Bangs said. "I need to be doing something."

The two of them went out into the snow. It took both of them to pull the door closed against the cold wind. Mr. Bangs soon came back with the wood.

Jim shoveled the snow away from the door. It was better to be working than sitting in the cabin.

The two of them stood by the cabin. The wind made a funny sound as it blew around the peaks above. Or was that the wind?

"Am I hearing things? That sounded like a cry—a cry for help," Jim said.

The sound came again. It was a cry!

"There is someone up there. Look! Do you see that black dot?" Mr. Bangs said.

Was it Ranger Don or Higgins coming back? Could it be one of the boys?

"Come on," Jim said. "Let's go. Someone is in trouble up there."

They pushed against the wind. Jim still carried his shovel. Snow covered the trail. They watched the black shape coming down the mountain. They moved as fast as they could. But the wind was against them.

"It's not Higgins or the ranger," Mr. Bangs said. "I think it's one of the boys!"

The boy up there was in trouble. Jim saw that he could not stay on his feet. Time and again, the boy fell. Each time, it was harder for him to get up again.

"Hold on!" Jim called. "We are coming."

The wind carried his call across the snow. The boy went down again. This time he did not get up. He lay there, not moving. They would reach him soon now.

All at once, Jim stopped. He heard a sound like thunder. The ground under his feet started to move. He looked up at the peak above with fear in his eyes.

"Get back! Get out of the way! A snow-slide!" he called to Mr. Bangs.

Down came the great wall of snow—pushing and thundering.

"The boy! He is right in the way of the slide!" Mr. Bangs said. "Let me go. I must go to him."

Snowslide!

Jim took Mr. Bangs' arm and pulled him back. The little man tried to get away.

"Let me go. Let me go, Jim. I have to get to that boy," he said.

But Jim held fast. "Hold on, Mr. Bangs. We can not help that boy if we are under a snowslide."

The black shape in the snow did not move. It was not far from Jim and Mr. Bangs. But the snowslide would go between them and the boy. On and on it came, pushing down from the peak. It hit the snow field below the peak. The snow field held much of the slide. But small parts broke away and moved slowly down. The thundering sound stopped.

"Now we can go after him!" Jim said.

The great slide had ended in a hill of snow. They could not see the boy on the other side.

Jim and Mr. Bangs went around the hill of snow. They moved up on the other side. They looked and looked for the boy.

"We should be close to him. But where is he?" Jim said. He was afraid.

All at once Mr. Bangs called out. "Look, Jim! Look there!"

They could see two legs above the snow. The slide had covered almost all of the boy.

They knew there was no time to talk now. Jim ran with his shovel. Mr. Bangs was close behind him. Jim worked fast. The snow flew as he pushed the shovel into the snow again and again. At last, they pulled the boy from the snow and turned him over.

Jim looked at the boy's white, still face. He was afraid to look at Mr. Bangs. Was this Andy?

But Mr. Bangs shook his head. "It is not my boy, Jim. Is he—will he—live?"

"We have got to make him live. Take his feet. Lay him face down," Jim said.

Jim took off his snowshoes. He got down in the snow with the boy's head between his legs. Jim's hands were on the boy's back, pushing—then letting go—then pulling up

on the boy's arms. Push—two—three. Pull—
two—three. On and on and on, he worked.

Still the boy made no sound. He did not
move. Jim began to be afraid. What if he
were doing this all wrong?

Mr. Bangs seemed to know what Jim was
feeling. "You are doing all right, Jim. Don't
give up, son. It takes time."

Jim knew Mr. Bangs was right. He could
not give up. He could not stop. The boy's life
was in his hands.

"I'll make it. I'll keep on trying!" he said.

Jim did not know how long he had worked
over the boy. Then all at once Jim knew he
could stop. The boy moved. He made a sound,
as if he were trying to talk.

"Come on. Let's take him back to the
cabin," Mr. Bangs said.

Together they picked the boy up. Slowly
they made their way back to the patrol cabin

with the boy. They took off his clothes. They put warm blankets around him.

"Put a chair under the end of the bed, Mr.Bangs. His head should be lower than his feet. And I wish we could get some of that coffee down him," Jim said slowly.

"We had better wait. I don't think he could take it now," said Mr. Bangs.

Together, Mr. Bangs and Jim worked over the boy. At last he opened his eyes. Mr.Bangs held his head and gave him coffee, a little at a time. The boy looked around the cabin. All at once, he sat up. He pushed Mr. Bangs away.

"Let me go. Let me go," the boy was crying. He started to pull off the blankets.

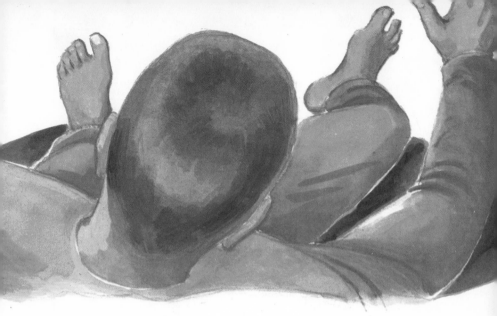

Jim ran to help Mr. Bangs. The two of them held the boy, but he tried to pull away.

"It's all right, son. You are safe. No one will hurt you," Mr. Bangs said over and over.

At last the boy was still again. He lay with his eyes open, but he did not seem to see anything.

Mr. Bangs turned to Jim. "The boy is out of his head, Jim," he said.

Wind thundered against the cabin door.

"How long must we wait before help comes?" thought Jim.

At the Foot of Dead Man's Peak

The wind blew hard on Dead Man's Peak. The ranger and Mr. Higgins pushed on. The clouds closed in around them. Cold snow blew into their faces. They had to stop for a time.

"We must have been climbing for over an hour," Mr. Higgins said.

"It's hard to tell where we are in this snow. But I don't think we have far to go now," the ranger said. "We should soon reach the foot of the main peak."

But now they could not see the wall of rock ahead. The snow was falling fast. The two men moved slowly and with great care.

The man in the helicopter had been wrong. It would take much more than an hour to reach the boys.

At last the snow began to let up. The heavy clouds slowly went away.

"It looks like we will make it after all," Ranger Don said. "Look over there!"

The great wall of rock was right ahead of them. At the foot of the rock, they could just make out the boy's shape.

Ranger Don called out, "Halloooh, up there!"

"Halloooh!" the answer came back.

The two men pushed on. The boy came down to them. He looked tired and afraid.

Ranger Don put an arm around him. "Are you all right, son? Where are the others?" he asked. "Where is Andy Bangs?"

"I am Andy. I am all right. But Bill is down there in that big crack. He hurt his leg when he fell. And Dick—Dick is gone," he said. There was fear in his eyes.

"I don't know what happened to him. He just went out of his head when Bill got hurt. He ran off down the mountain. I tried to stop him. But I could not leave Bill here."

Ranger Don and Higgins ran to the crack
and looked down. Bill lay on a shelf about
ten feet below. His eyes were closed and his
face was white. From the way his leg was

turned, the ranger knew that it must be broken.

"How long has he been there? Has he talked at all?" Higgins asked.

"He fell last night. I have tried to keep him talking. There was food in the things that the helicopter dropped. He ate a little of it. He has been sleeping about an hour now," Andy said.

"Help me with the litter," Ranger Don said to Higgins.

The two men moved the litter to the crack. The litter was made of two poles with wire between. There was a rope at each end. Ranger Don took one rope, and Higgins took the other. Slowly, they lowered the litter down into the crack.

They felt the litter come to a stop on the shelf below.

"All right. I will go down after the boy," said Ranger Don.

He fixed his rope and slowly lowered himself down into the crack. He held on to one side of the rock wall as he went down. Higgins and Andy held the other end of the rope. They let it out slowly.

Ranger Don felt for the shelf with his foot. "All right," he called to them at last. "I am all the way down."

The men slowly let out more rope for the ranger.

He moved slowly along the shelf, holding the rope. Part of the shelf gave way under his foot. He would have to stay close to the wall of the crack. There would not be much room to work. At last he reached the boy.

"Bill," he said. "This is no time to sleep!" Slowly the boy's eyes opened. He saw the ranger.

"I am glad you are here," was all he could say.

"Send down the first-aid things," Ranger Don called up to Higgins. "I am going to have to fix Bill's leg before I can move him."

Soon the first-aid things came down on a rope. The ranger worked fast.

"Hold on, Bill. This will hurt. I will have to put something under this broken leg to hold it still. The doctor can fix it later."

The boy's face went white. He did not cry out. Soon the job was done. Ranger Don sent the first-aid things up on the rope. Then he moved Bill on to the litter.

"I will go up first, Bill. Then I can help pull you up," Ranger Don said.

He pushed against the wall with his feet as Higgins and Andy pulled. They pulled him up out of the crack.

"Now, for the litter," Higgins said. "The ranger and I will take the ropes." Slowly they pulled the litter up the wall.

"Here it comes. Over the top," Andy said. He helped to pull up the litter.

"Let's have the blankets that came with the litter, Higgins. Bill is going to need them," Ranger Don said. He put blankets around the boy.

"Bill seems to be in good shape," Higgins said. "I think he will be all right, if we can reach the cabin soon. I will pack the things, and we can get started."

"Yes. We should leave as soon as we can. You pack up. I will radio the main station that we are coming down," the ranger said.

Mr. Higgins soon had things packed. Ranger Don telephoned the main station and they were ready to start.

Mr. Higgins said, "I had a look at Andy's hands. I don't like the look of them, ranger. He says he can't feel a thing. I think his hands are frozen."

"Higgins, we can't take care of him here. We must get to the patrol cabin. The storm is getting bad. The main station says it will hit hard very soon. We are going to have to move and move fast!" the ranger said.

Back Down the Trail

Ranger Don looked at Andy Bangs. The boy was trying to fix his rope. His hands were stiff, but he worked and worked. At last, the rope was fixed. Andy looked up. He saw the ranger watching him.

"I know what you are thinking, ranger," Andy said. "But don't worry. I will make out

all right. I got us into this. I will do my part
to get us out of it."

"Good boy, Andy," said Ranger Don. "We
will need your help. Higgins and I will take
the litter. You take the pole and go first.
Watch out for cracks."

Ranger Don and Higgins picked up the
litter. Andy started off with the pole. Snow
was falling now. At times it blew around
them in great clouds. The deep snow under
their feet made the going hard.

"Keep to your right, Andy," Ranger Don called. "Keep your eye on those two black rocks. We will head down between them."

The cold wind blew down from the peaks above. It blew harder and harder. It blew snow into the ranger's face and eyes. At times, he could not see Andy Bangs, a few feet ahead of him. Then all at once the ranger felt a strong pull on the rope.

Andy had gone down. Ranger Don pulled back on the rope to keep from falling. He almost lost his hold on the litter. The move hurt Bill, and he let out a cry.

"What is wrong?" Higgins called over the wind.

"Andy is down. Hold on," the ranger called back. He put the litter down. Slowly, he felt his way along the rope.

"Watch out," Andy called. "Don't come too close. There is a crack here."

The boy lay in the snow. Slowly, he pulled himself along with his arms. The ranger pulled on the rope. At last, Andy was on safe ground. The ranger helped him to his feet again.

"Wow! That was close," Andy said. He looked at the place where his foot had gone through the snow.

"Maybe you had better go first, ranger. I can help with the litter."

Ranger Don looked at the snow that blew around them. He could just see the two black rocks that were in the trail ahead. The storm was very bad now. There was danger of going off the trail.

"You are right, Andy," the ranger said. "It would be best if I could go first. But what about those hands of yours? Can you hold the litter?"

"I will be all right, ranger," Andy said. He took the ranger's place at one end of the litter. Ranger Don looked at all the ropes again. Then he took the pole and started off ahead.

The litter was heavy. Bill's leg was hurting

him. He began to cry out and turn from side
to side. Higgins and Andy almost lost their
hold on the litter. Again and again they almost went down in the deep snow. But there
was no time to stop. They had to reach the
patrol cabin before dark. And all of them
knew it.

They pushed on and on through the storm.
At last the two black rocks were behind

them. They moved across the snow fields above the cabin. Here the great snowslide had covered part of the trail.

It was almost night when they saw the cabin. They were too tired to call out. It was all they could do to take the last few steps. At last Ranger Don fell against the cabin door.

"Jim! Jim, let us in," Ranger Don called. . The door opened and he heard Jim cry, "They are here!"

Jim and Mr. Bangs pulled the ranger into the cabin. They ran to take the litter from Higgins and Andy.

"Andy, Andy, my boy!" Mr. Bangs said, putting his arms around the boy. "Go in the cabin where it is warm. Let me take that litter."

Jim took one end of the litter. Higgins made it into the cabin and dropped into a chair. But Andy just stood still, holding his end of the litter.

"I—I can't let go. It is my hands. They are frozen stiff," he said.

Mr. Bangs looked down at his son's hands. He took the litter from Andy.

"Thanks, Dad," Andy said. He held up his frozen hands and looked at them. "I would give them both if only Dick were safe. But he is gone, Dad. He is dead. ·And it is my doing. I can never get over it."

"Dick is well and safe, son. He is in the cabin. Now, go on in," Mr. Bangs said.

He watched the boy hurry into the cabin. He heard Andy's cry, "Dick! You are safe!"

Mr. Bangs thought of little Joe Higgins, waiting down the mountain. He knew now why Higgins had gone after the boys—why he had to go. He knew, too, why Higgins would not take the money.

A Last Look at the Peak

All night long the storm thundered about the little cabin on the mountain.

Jim looked at the tired faces around him. "Oh, if this storm would only end," he thought. "We must have help soon!"

74

When the storm ended, the helicopter could come. It could take Andy and Bill to a doctor. Both boys were in need of a doctor's care.

It was a long night for all of them in the little cabin. There was sleep for no one.

There was nothing to do but wait and listen to the wind. It seemed that morning would never come.

Jim heard Andy talking to his father. "I am sorry, Dad, for all the trouble I made."

"Don't try to talk now, son," Mr. Bangs said. "You can tell me about it later."

"No. I want to tell you now." Andy talked very slowly. The feeling was coming back to his hands. They were starting to hurt.

"I wanted to get to the top of that mountain, Dad. You will never know how much," Andy said. "You made things so easy for me —too easy. All my life you gave me what you thought I wanted. I know I should have been glad. But what I wanted more than anything was to work for things. I wanted to do something hard—just to show that I could."

"Andy, I think I know what you are talking about," said Mr. Bangs slowly. "But what did you show by climbing this mountain?"

"Nothing," Andy said. "It was a foolish thing to do. I can see that now. I don't know how to tell you how sorry I am."

Mr. Bangs put his hand on the boy's arm. "There are a lot of ways for a man to show what he can do, son. Now that I know how you feel, I will never stand in your way again."

"Thanks, Dad. After this, I will work for things," Andy said. "And I will not be so foolish again."

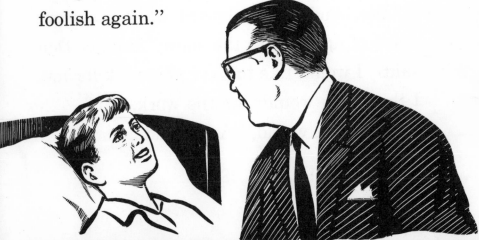

Ranger Don came over to Andy's bed.

"Well, Andy," he said. "What do you think about mountain climbing now?"

Andy shook his head. "It's a funny thing," he said, "but I would still like to see what the world looks like from the top of this mountain."

The ranger laughed. "Come back next summer. Jim and I will take you up. And if you are looking for hard work, why don't you work for Big Pines next summer?"

"Do you—would you let me work here? After all the trouble I made for you?" Andy asked. He looked at the ranger and then at his father.

"Yes, Andy. You showed what you were made of up there in the snow," Ranger Don said. "I would like to have you work for me. I think you would like the work, too."

"I know I would," Andy said.

Jim had been listening to Andy and the men talk. He had stopped listening to the wind. Now, all at once, he jumped to his feet.

"Uncle Don, listen! The wind has stopped. The storm must be over," Jim said.

He ran to the cabin door and pulled it open. The snow was deep against the cabin door. But the wind was gone. The heavy black clouds were gone. Jim could see the sun coming up behind Dead Man's Peak.

As he stood there, he heard the telephone ring. It must be the call they were all waiting for.

Ranger Don turned from the telephone. "That was the main ranger station calling. The helicopter is on the way. It will be here soon."

At last help was coming! Tired as they were, the men went to work. Higgins and Jim took shovels and began to move the snow from the cabin door. Mr. Bangs and the ranger got the boys ready for their trip in the helicopter.

"Here it comes!" Jim called.

The little black dot in the sky came closer
and closer. At last it stopped above the cabin.
Slowly it came down upon the snow.

Higgins and the ranger carried Bill's litter
to the helicopter. Then they helped Andy and
Dick out of the cabin. Bill and Andy were
laughing and talking. But Dick had nothing
to say. He sat by himself and turned away
from the others.

Higgins, Mr. Bangs, Jim, and the ranger
stood watching as the helicopter flew slowly
away.

"The boys are going to be all right, Mr. Bangs. Try not to worry," the ranger said.

"It's not Andy and Bill I am worrying about," said Mr. Bangs. "It's Dick. Do you think he will be all right?"

"It will be a hard thing for Dick to get over," the ranger said slowly.

They turned and went back into the cabin. Mr. Higgins began to get his things together. He wanted to hurry. He wanted to tell Joe that the boys were safe.

"I know you would like to go to Andy," Ranger Don said to Mr. Bangs. "You may as well go down with Higgins. Jim and I have some work to do here. We will come later."

Higgins and Andy's father were soon ready to start. Mr. Bangs shook hands with Jim and Ranger Don.

"Good-by, ranger. Good-by, Jim. How can I thank you for what you have done? You will not let me give you anything. So all I can do is say 'thank you.' It seems so little— for bringing my boy back."

"It's all part of the job," the ranger said. "Knowing Andy, Bill, and Dick are safe is all the thanks I need. Good-by."

Ranger Don put his arm around Jim. Together, they watched Higgins and Mr. Bangs go off down the trail.

"Well, Jim. We had better get to work here," said Ranger Don.

They went into the patrol cabin. Jim took the blankets from the beds. He put them up on the wires to keep them from the rats. Here the rats could not eat them. The last thing the ranger did was to see that there was food under the floor. Jim knew they had to leave the room just as they had found it.

At last they closed the cabin door.

Jim took one last look at Dead Man's Peak. With the sun above it, the snow looked very white.

"You know something, Uncle Don! I think I would like to climb Dead Man's Peak. It must be a good feeling to climb all the way to the top. I would like to see what the world looks like from up there," Jim said.

Ranger Don laughed. "To me it looks like a very good world from right here, Jim. But, I'll take you up there next summer," he said.

"It will be next summer before my feet are warm again," Jim laughed.

The ranger put his arm around Jim. "Me, too," he said. "Come on, boy. Let's go."

Together, they started down the trail.

WORD LIST

WORD LIST

The total number of running words in *Jim Forest and Dead Man's Peak* is 8,325, and the number of different words used is 419. Of these, 396 should be familiar to children reading at the second-grade level. The remaining 23 words, which are above second-grade level but necessary to the context of the story, are listed below according to the page on which they first occur. Words introduced in *Jim Forest and Ranger Don*, *Jim Forest and the Bandits* and *Jim Forest and the Mystery Hunter*, the first three books of the series, are starred.

1	ranger*	27	—	56	—
2	peak	28	—	57	—
	pines*	29	—	58	—
	station*	30	helicopter	59	—
3	—	31	—	60	—
4	patrol	32	moving	61	—
	snowshoes	33	—	62	—
5	map*	34	—	63	—
	slowly	35	—	64	—
6	kit	36	—	65	—
7	—	37	thundered*	66	—
8	worry	38	flare	67	—
9	—	39	—	68	—
10	—	40	aid	69	—
11	valley		litter	70	—
12	job*	41	—	71	—
13	—	42	—	72	—
14	lodge	43	—	73	—
15	—	44	—	74	—
16	trail*	45	shovel	75	—
17	—	46	—	76	—
18	—	47	—	77	—
19	—	48	snowslide	78	—
20	—	49	—	79	—
21	—	50	—	80	—
22	wires	51	—	81	—
23	—	52	—	82	—
24	—	53	—	83	—
25	—	54	—	84	—
26	—	55	—	85	—